ZLATEH THE GOAT
AND OTHER STORIES

ZLATEH THE GOAT

and Other Stories

by
ISAAC BASHEVIS SINGER

Pictures by MAURICE SENDAK

Translated from the Yiddish
by the Author and Elizabeth Shub

Harper & Row, Publishers · Established 1817

Contents

Illustrations

Foreword

CHILDREN are as puzzled by passing time as grown-ups. What happens to a day once it is gone? Where are all our yesterdays with their joys and sorrows? Literature helps us remember the past with its many moods. To the storyteller yesterday is still here as are the years and the decades gone by.

In stories time does not vanish. Neither do men and animals. For the writer and his readers all creatures go on living forever. What happened long ago is still present.

It is in this spirit that I wrote these tales. In real life many of the people that I describe no longer exist, but to me they remain alive and I hope they will amuse the reader with their wisdom, their strange beliefs, and sometimes with their foolishness.

I dedicate this book to the many children who had no chance to grow up because of stupid wars and cruel persecutions which devastated cities and destroyed innocent families. I hope that when the readers of these stories become men and women they will love not only their own children but all good children everywhere.

I. B. S.

ZLATEH THE GOAT
AND OTHER STORIES

Fool's Paradise

FOOL'S PARADISE

SOMEWHERE, sometime, there lived a rich man whose name was Kadish. He had an only son who was called Atzel. In the household of Kadish there lived a distant relative, an orphan girl, called Aksah. Atzel was a tall boy with black hair and black eyes. Aksah was somewhat shorter than Atzel, and she had blue eyes and golden hair. Both were about the same age. As children, they ate together, studied together, played together. Atzel played the husband; Aksah, his wife. It was taken for granted that when they grew up they would really marry.

But when they had grown up, Atzel suddenly became ill. It was a sickness no one had ever heard of before: Atzel imagined that he was dead.

How did such an idea come to him? It seems it came from listening to stories about paradise. He had had an old nurse who had constantly described the place to him. She had told him that in paradise it was not necessary to work or to study or make any effort whatsoever. In paradise one ate the meat of wild oxen and the flesh of whales; one drank the wine that the Lord reserved for the just; one slept late into the day; and one had no duties.

Atzel was lazy by nature. He hated to get up early in the morning and to study languages and science. He knew that one day he would have to take over his father's business and he did not want to.

Since his old nurse had told Atzel that the only way to get to paradise was to die, he had made up his mind to do just that as quickly as possible. He thought and brooded about it so much that soon he began to imagine that he *was* dead.

Of course his parents became terribly worried when they saw what was happening to Atzel. Aksah cried in secret. The family did everything possible to try to convince Atzel that he was alive, but he refused to believe them. He would say, "Why don't you bury me? You see that I am dead. Because of you I cannot get to paradise."

Many doctors were called in to examine Atzel, and all tried to convince the boy that he was alive. They pointed out that he was talking, eating, and sleeping. But before long Atzel began to eat less and he rarely spoke. His family feared that he would die.

In despair Kadish went to consult a great specialist, celebrated for his knowledge and wisdom. His name was Dr. Yoetz. After listening to a description of Atzel's illness, he said to Kadish, "I promise to cure your son in eight days, on one condition. You must do whatever I tell you to, no matter how strange it may seem."

Kadish agreed, and Dr. Yoetz said he would visit Atzel that same day. Kadish went home to prepare the household. He told his wife, Aksah, and the servants that all were to follow the doctor's orders without question, and they did so.

When Dr. Yoetz arrived, he was taken to Atzel's room. The boy lay on his bed, pale and thin from fasting, his hair disheveled, his nightclothes wrinkled.

The doctor took one look at Atzel and called out, "Why do you keep a dead body in the house? Why don't you make a funeral?"

On hearing these words the parents became terribly frightened, but Atzel's face lit up with a smile and he said, "You see, I was right."

Although Kadish and his wife were bewildered by the doctor's words, they remembered Kadish's promise, and went immediately to make arrangements for the funeral.

Atzel now became so excited by what the doctor had said that he jumped out of bed and began to dance and clap his hands. His joy made him hungry and he asked for food. But Dr. Yoetz replied, "Wait, you will eat in paradise."

The doctor requested that a room be prepared to look like paradise. The walls were hung with white satin, and precious rugs covered the floors. The windows were shuttered, and draperies tightly drawn. Candles and oil lamps burned day and night. The servants were dressed in white with wings on their backs and were to play angels.

Atzel was placed in an open coffin, and a funeral ceremony was held. Atzel was so exhausted with happiness that he slept right through it. When he awoke, he found himself in a room he didn't recognize. "Where am I?" he asked.

"In paradise, my lord," a winged servant replied.

"I'm terribly hungry," Atzel said. "I'd like some whale flesh and sacred wine."

"In a moment, my lord."

The chief servant clapped his hands and a door opened through which there came men servants and maids, all with wings on their backs, bearing golden trays laden with meat, fish, pomegranates and persimmons, pineapples and peaches. A tall servant with a long white beard carried a golden goblet full of wine. Atzel was so starved that he ate ravenously. The angels hovered around him, filling his plate and goblet even before he had time to ask for more.

When he had finished eating, Atzel declared he wanted to rest. Two angels undressed and bathed him. Then they brought him a nightdress of fine embroidered linen, placed a nightcap with a tassel on his head, and carried him to a bed with silken sheets and a purple velvet canopy. Atzel immediately fell into a deep and happy sleep.

When he awoke, it was morning but it could just as well have been night. The shutters were closed, and the candles and oil lamps were burning. As soon as the servants saw that Atzel was awake, they brought in exactly the same meal as the day before.

"Why do you give me the same food as yesterday?"

8

Atzel asked. "Don't you have any milk, coffee, fresh rolls, and butter?"

"No, my lord. In paradise one always eats the same food," the servant replied.

"Is it already day, or is it still night?" Atzel asked.

"In paradise there is neither day nor night."

Dr. Yoetz had given careful instructions on how the servants were to talk to Atzel and behave toward him.

Atzel again ate the fish, meat, fruit, and drank the wine, but his appetite was not as good as it had been. When he had finished his meal and washed his hands in a golden finger bowl, he asked, "What time is it?"

"In paradise time does not exist," the servant answered.

"What shall I do now?" Atzel questioned.

"In paradise, my lord, one doesn't do anything."

"Where are the other saints?" Atzel inquired. "I'd like to meet them."

"In paradise each family has a place of its own."

"Can't one go visiting?"

"In paradise the dwellings are too far from each other for visiting. It would take thousands of years to go from one to the other."

"When will my family come?" Atzel asked.

"Your father still has twenty years to live, your mother thirty. And as long as they live they can't come here."

"What about Aksah?"

"She has more than fifty years to live."

"Do I have to be alone all that time?"

"Yes, my lord."

For a while Atzel shook his head, pondering. Then he asked, "What is Aksah going to do?"

"Right now, she's mourning for you. But you know, my lord, that one cannot mourn forever. Sooner or later she will forget you, meet another young man, and marry. That's how it is with the living."

Atzel got up and began to walk to and fro. His long sleep and the rich food had restored his energy. For the first time in years lazy Atzel had a desire to do something, but there was nothing to do in his paradise.

For eight days Atzel remained in his false heaven, and from day to day he became sadder and sadder. He missed his father; he longed for his mother; he yearned for Aksah. Idleness did not appeal to him as it had in former times. Now he wished he had something to study; he dreamed of traveling; he wanted to ride his horse, to talk to friends. The food, which had so delighted him the first day, lost its flavor.

The time came when he could no longer conceal his sadness. He remarked to one of the servants, "I see now that it is not as bad to live as I had thought."

"To live, my lord, is difficult. One has to study, work, do business. Here everything is easy," the servant consoled him.

"I would rather chop wood and carry stones than sit here. And how long will this last?"

"Forever."

"Stay here forever?" Atzel began to tear his hair in grief. "I'd rather kill myself."

"A dead man cannot kill himself."

On the eighth day, when it seemed that Atzel had reached the deepest despair, one of the servants, as had been arranged, came to him and said, "My lord, there

has been a mistake. You are not dead. You must leave paradise."

"I'm alive?"

"Yes, you are alive, and I will bring you back to earth."

Atzel was beside himself with joy. The servant blindfolded him, and after leading him back and forth through the long corridors of the house, brought him to the room where his family was waiting and uncovered his eyes.

It was a bright day, and the sun shone through the open windows. A breeze from the surrounding fields and orchards freshened the air. In the garden outside, the birds were singing and the bees buzzing as they flew from flower to flower. From the barns and stables Atzel could hear the mooing of cows and the neighing of horses. Joyfully he embraced and kissed his parents and Aksah.

"I didn't know how good it was to be alive," he cried out.

And to Aksah he said: "Haven't you met another young man while I was away? Do you still love me?"

"Yes, I do, Atzel. I could not forget you."

"If that is so, it is time we got married."

It was not long before the wedding took place. Dr. Yoetz was the guest of honor. Musicians played; guests came from faraway cities. Some came on horseback, some drove mules, and some rode camels. All brought fine gifts for the bride and groom, in gold, silver, ivory, and assorted precious stones. The celebration lasted seven days and seven nights. It was one of the gayest weddings that old men had ever remembered. Atzel and Aksah were extremely happy, and both lived to a ripe old age. Atzel stopped being lazy and became the most diligent merchant in the whole region. His trading caravans traveled as far as Baghdad and India.

It was not until after the wedding that Atzel learned how Dr. Yoetz had cured him, and that he had lived in a fool's paradise. In the years to come he often talked with Aksah about his adventures, and later they told the tale of Dr. Yoetz's wonderful cure to their children and grandchildren, always finishing with the words, "But, of course, what paradise is really like, no one can tell."

Grandmother's Tale

GRANDMOTHER'S TALE

IT'S GREAT fun to play dreidel. But children must go to sleep. That is what Grandmother Leah had said. They begged her to tell them a story first.

Once upon a time a father had four sons and four daughters. The sons wore earlocks, the girls, braids. Standing next to each other, they looked like the steps of a ladder. It was Hanukkah, and after the candles were lit, they all got Hanukkah money and sat down to play dreidel, forgetting about bedtime. Mother and father reminded them that it was getting late. But the children who were winning wanted to win more, and those who were losing wanted to win back what they had lost. Suddenly there was a knock at the door. In came a young man with sideburns and a curled moustache. He wore a coat lined with fox fur, a hat with a feather in it, high boots with spurs. He was covered with snow, but he looked gay and untroubled. He had lost his way in the blizzard, he said. Could he stay till morning?

Outside stood his sleigh. It was adorned with carved ivory, was drawn by four white horses, and the reins shone with jewels. The boys unharnessed the horses, took them into the stable, and fed them hay and oats. They asked the guest if he were hungry. "Like a wolf," he replied. Would he join them in playing dreidel? "Gladly," he said, and sat down at the table to play with them.

He ate pancakes with cinnamon, drank tea with jam, and puffed smoke rings from his amber pipe. He staked silver coins and lost them. He put out gold coins and lost them too. For everybody else the dreidel stopped on Gimel, for him it always fell on Nun. He lost and laughed, lost again and joked. He drank wine and mead, and his purse seemed to have no bottom. Midnight had passed and bedtime was forgotten. Dogs barked in the night, roosters crowed, hens cackled, crows cawed, geese honked, ducks quacked. In the stable the horses neighed and stamped their hooves on the ground.

"What's wrong with our animals tonight?" the oldest boy asked. At that moment he looked at the wall and noticed that there were only eight shadows instead of nine. The stranger did not cast a shadow. Now everything was clear. It is known that devils cast no shadows. Their guest was not a man but a demon. When the clock struck thirteen times, there was no longer any doubt who the stranger really was.

The stranger saw by the children's frightened faces that

22

his secret was out. He rose with a loud laugh, stuck his tongue out to his belly, and grew twice as tall. Horns came from behind his ears, and there he stood, a devil. Before anyone could say a word, he began to spin like a dreidel, round and round, and the house spun with him. The Hanukkah lamp swayed, plates clattered to the floor which shook like a ship on a stormy sea. The devil whistled. Mice appeared, and goblins in red caps and green boots whirled around in a ring, laughing and screaming. Suddenly the devil sprouted wings, clapped them together, "Cock-a-doodle-doo," and the whole company disappeared.

> *Gold and silver turned to dust,*
> *In the snow a track of rust,*
> *Gone the treasure on the bench,*
> *Nothing left but devil's stench.*
> *Elflocks in the children's hair,*
> *Devil's dirt was everywhere.*
> *Good the devil's gone away*
> *With his horses and his sleigh.*
> *Such a pity, such a shame,*
> *Hanukkah night and a devil's game.*

This is the story told by Grandmother Leah as she knitted a sock for her youngest grandchild.

"Grandma, Grandma, tell us more," the children pleaded. But Grandmother Leah kissed their heads and said it was time to go to sleep. "Tomorrow, children, is another day. There will be a new candle in the Hanukkah lamp, fresh snow on the ground, and I will tell you another story."

23

The Snow In Chelm

THE SNOW IN CHELM

CHELM was a village of fools, fools young and old. One night someone spied the moon reflected in a barrel of water. The people of Chelm imagined it had fallen in. They sealed the barrel so that the moon would not escape. When the barrel was opened in the morning and the moon wasn't there, the villagers decided it had been stolen. They sent for the police, and when the thief couldn't be found, the fools of Chelm cried and moaned.

Of all the fools of Chelm, the most famous were its seven Elders. Because they were the village's oldest and greatest fools, they ruled in Chelm. They had white beards and high foreheads from too much thinking.

29

Once, on a Hanukkah night, the snow fell all evening. It covered all of Chelm like a silver tablecloth. The moon shone; the stars twinkled; the snow shimmered like pearls and diamonds.

That evening the seven Elders were sitting and pondering, wrinkling their foreheads. The village was in need of money, and they did not know where to get it. Suddenly the oldest of them all, Gronam the Great Fool, exclaimed, "The snow is silver!"

"I see pearls in the snow!" another shouted.

"And I see diamonds!" a third called out.

It became clear to the Elders of Chelm that a treasure had fallen from the sky.

But soon they began to worry. The people of Chelm liked to go walking, and they would most certainly trample the treasure. What was to be done? Silly Tudras had an idea.

"Let's send a messenger to knock on all the windows and let the people know that they must remain in their houses until all the silver, all the pearls, and all the diamonds are safely gathered up."

For a while the Elders were satisfied. They rubbed their hands in approval of the clever idea. But then Dopey Lekisch called out in consternation, "The messenger himself will trample the treasure."

The Elders realized that Lekisch was right, and again they wrinkled their high foreheads in an effort to solve the problem.

"I've got it!" exclaimed Shmerel the Ox.

"Tell us, tell us," pleaded the Elders.

"The messenger must not go on foot. He must be car-

30

ried on a table so that his feet will not tread on the precious snow."

Everybody was delighted with Shmerel the Ox's solution; and the Elders, clapping their hands, admired their own wisdom.

The Elders immediately sent to the kitchen for Gimpel the errand boy and stood him on a table. Now who was going to carry the table? It was lucky that in the kitchen there were Treitle the cook, Berel the potato peeler, Yukel the salad mixer, and Yontel, who was in charge of the community goat. All four were ordered to lift up the table on which Gimpel stood. Each one took hold of a leg. On top stood Gimpel, grasping a wooden hammer with which to tap on the villagers' windows. Off they went.

At each window Gimpel knocked with the hammer and called out, "No one leaves the house tonight. A treasure has fallen from the sky, and it is forbidden to step on it."

The people of Chelm obeyed the Elders and remained in their houses all night. Meanwhile the Elders themselves sat up trying to figure out how to make the best use of the treasure once it had been gathered up.

Silly Tudras proposed that they sell it and buy a goose which lays golden eggs. Thus the community would be provided with a steady income.

Dopey Lekisch had another idea. Why not buy eyeglasses that make things look bigger for all the inhabitants of Chelm? Then the houses, the streets, the stores would all look bigger, and of course if Chelm *looked* bigger, then it *would be* bigger. It would no longer be a village, but a big city.

33

There were other, equally clever ideas. But while the Elders were weighing their various plans, morning came and the sun rose. They looked out of the window, and, alas, they saw the snow had been trampled. The heavy boots of the table carriers had destroyed the treasure.

The Elders of Chelm clutched at their white beards and admitted to one another that they had made a mistake. Perhaps, they reasoned, four others should have carried the four men who had carried the table that held Gimpel the errand boy?

After long deliberations the Elders decided that if next Hanukkah a treasure would again fall down from the sky, that is exactly what they would do.

Although the villagers remained without a treasure, they were full of hope for the next year and praised their Elders, who they knew could always be counted on to find a way, no matter how difficult the problem.

The Mixed-Up Feet
and The Silly Bridegroom

THE MIXED-UP FEET
AND THE SILLY BRIDEGROOM

NEAR THE VILLAGE of Chelm there was a hamlet called East Chelm, where there lived a tenant farmer called Shmelka and his wife, Shmelkicha. They had four daughters, all of whom slept in the same broad bed. Their names were Yenta, Pesha, Trina, Yachna.

As a rule the girls got up early in the morning to milk the cows and help their mother with the household chores. But one winter morning they stayed in bed later than usual. When their mother came to see what was keeping them, she found all four struggling and scream- ing in the bed. Shmelkicha demanded to know what all the commotion was about and why they were pulling each other's hair. The girls replied that in their sleep they had gotten their feet mixed up, and now they didn't know whose feet belonged to whom, and so of course they couldn't get up.

As soon as she learned about her daughters' mixed-up feet, Shmelkicha, who was from Chelm proper, became exceedingly frightened. She remembered that a similar event had taken place in Chelm many years before and, oh, how much trouble there had been. She ran at once to a neighbor and begged her to milk the cows, and she herself set off for Chelm to ask the town's Elder what to do. Before she left, she said to the girls, "You stay in bed and don't budge until I return. Because once you get up with the wrong feet, it will be very difficult to set things right."

When Shmelkicha arrived in Chelm and told the Elder about what had happened to her daughters, he clutched his white beard with one hand, placed the other on his forehead, and was immediately lost in thought. As he pondered he hummed a Chelm melody.

After a while he said, "There is no perfect solution for a case of mixed-up feet. But there is something that sometimes helps."

He told Shmelkicha to take a long stick, walk into the girls' room, and unexpectedly whack the blanket where their feet were. "It is possible," explained the wise Elder, "that in surprise and pain each girl will grab at her own feet and jump out of bed." A similar remedy had once been used in such a case, and it had worked.

Many townspeople were present when the Elder made his pronouncement, and as always they admired his great wisdom. The Elder stated further that in order to prevent such an accident in the future, it would be advisable to gradually marry off the girls. Once each girl was married and had her own house and her own husband, there would be no danger that they would get their feet mixed up again.

Shmelkicha returned to East Chelm, picked up a stick, walked into her daughters' room, and whacked the quilt with all her might. The girls were completely taken aback, but before a moment had passed, they were out of bed, screaming in pain and fright, each jumping on her own feet. Shmelka, their father, and a number of neighbors who had followed Shmelkicha into the house and witnessed what had happened, again came to the conclusion that the wisdom of the Elder of Chelm knew no bounds.

Shmelka and Shmelkicha immediately decided to carry out the rest of the Elder's advice and started looking for a husband for their eldest daughter. They soon found a young man of Chelm called Lemel. His father was a coachman, and Lemel himself already owned a horse and wagon. It was clear that Yenta's future husband would be a good provider.

When they brought the couple together to sign the marriage agreement, Yenta began to cry bitterly. Asked why she was crying, she replied, "Lemel is a stranger, and I don't want to marry a stranger."

"Didn't I marry a stranger?" her mother asked.

"You married Father," Yenta answered, "and I have to marry a total stranger." And her face became wet with tears.

The match would have come to nothing, but luckily

they had invited the Elder of Chelm to be present. And, after some pondering, he again found the way out. He said to Yenta, "Sign the marriage contract. The moment you sign it, Lemel becomes your betrothed. And when you marry, you will not be marrying a stranger, you will be marrying your betrothed."

When Yenta heard these words, she was overjoyed. Lemel kissed the Elder three times on his huge forehead, and the rest of the company praised the wisdom of the Elder of Chelm, which was even greater than that of wise King Solomon.

But now a new problem arose. Neither Lemel nor Yenta had learned to sign their names.

Again the Elder came to the rescue: "Let Yenta make three small circles on the paper, and Lemel three dashes. These will serve as their signatures and seal the contract."

Yenta and Lemel did as the Elder ordered, and everybody was gay and happy. Shmelkicha treated all the witnesses to cheese blintzes and borscht, and the first plate naturally went to the Elder of Chelm, whose appetite was particularly good that day.

Before Lemel returned to Chelm proper, from where he had driven in his own horse and wagon, Shmelka gave him as a gift a small penknife with a mother-of-pearl handle. It happened to be the first day of Hanukkah, and the penknife was both an engagement gift and a Hanukkah present.

Since Lemel often came to East Chelm to buy from the peasants the milk, butter, hay, oats, and flax which he sold to the townspeople of Chelm, he soon came to visit Yenta again. Shmelka asked Lemel whether his friends in

Chelm had liked his penknife, and Lemel replied that they had never seen it.

"Why not?" Shmelka asked.

"Because I lost it."

"How did you lose it?"

"I put the penknife into the wagon and it got lost in the hay."

Shmelka was not a native of Chelm but came from another nearby town, and he said to Lemel, "You don't put a penknife into a wagon full of straw and hay and with cracks and holes in the bottom to boot. A penknife you place in your pocket, and then it does not get lost."

"Future Father-in-law, you are right," Lemel answered. "Next time I will know what to do."

Since the first gift had been lost, Shmelka gave Lemel a jar of freshly fried chicken fat to replace it. Lemel thanked him and returned to Chelm.

Several days later, when business again brought Lemel to East Chelm, Yenta's parents noticed that his coat pocket was torn, and the entire left side of his coat was covered with grease stains.

"What happened to your coat?" Shmelkicha asked.

Lemel replied, "I put the jar of chicken fat in my pocket, but the road is full of holes and ditches and I could not help bumping against the side of the wagon. The jar broke, and it tore my pocket and the fat ran out all over my clothes."

"Why did you put the jar of chicken fat into your pocket?" Shmelka asked.

"Didn't you tell me to?"

"A penknife you put into your pocket. A jar of chicken

fat you wrap in paper and place in the hay so that it will not break."

Lemel replied, "Next time I will know what to do."

Since Lemel had had little use out of the first two gifts, Yenta herself gave him a silver gulden, which her father had given her as a Hanukkah gift.

When Lemel came to the hamlet again, he was asked how he had spent the money.

"I lost it," he replied.

"How did you lose it?"

"I wrapped it in paper and placed it in the hay. But when I arrived in Chelm and unloaded my merchandise, the gulden was gone."

"A gulden is not a jar of chicken fat," Shmelka informed him. "A gulden you put into your purse."

"Next time I will know what to do."

Before Lemel returned to Chelm, Yenta gave her fiancé some newly laid eggs, still warm from the chickens.

On his next visit he was asked how he had enjoyed the eggs, and he replied that they had all been broken.

"How did they break?"

"I put them into my purse, but when I tried to close it, the eggs broke."

"Nobody puts eggs into a purse," Shmelka said. "Eggs you put into a basket bedded with straw and covered with a rag so that they will not break."

"Next time I will know what to do."

Since Lemel had not been able to enjoy the gifts he had received, Yenta decided to present him with a live duck.

When he returned, he was asked how the duck was

faring, and he said she had died on the way to Chelm.

"How did she die?"

"I placed her in a basket with straw and covered it well with rags, just as you had told me to. When I arrived home, the duck was dead."

"A duck has to breathe," Shmelkicha said. "If you cover her with rags, she will suffocate. A duck you put in a cage, with some corn to eat, and then she will arrive safely."

"Next time I will know what to do."

Since Lemel had gained neither use nor pleasure from any of his gifts, Yenta decided to give him her goldfish, a pet she had had for several years.

And again on his return, when asked about the gold-fish, he replied that it was dead.

"Why is it dead?"

"I placed it in a cage and gave it some corn, but when I arrived it was dead."

Since Lemel was still without a gift, Yenta decided to give him her canary, which she loved dearly. But Shmelka told her that it seemed pointless to give Lemel any more gifts, because whatever you gave him either died or got lost. Instead Shmelka and Shmelkicha decided to get the advice of the Elder of Chelm.

The Elder listened to the whole story, and as usual clutched his long white beard with one hand and placed the other on his high forehead.

After much pondering and humming, he proclaimed, "The road between East Chelm and Chelm is fraught with all kinds of dangers, and that is why such misfortunes occur. The best thing to do is to have a quick marriage. Then Lemel and Yenta will be together, and Lemel will not have to drag his gifts from one place to another, and no misfortunes will befall them."

This advice pleased everyone, and the marriage was soon celebrated. All the peasants of the hamlet of East Chelm and half of the townspeople of Chelm danced and rejoiced at the wedding. Before the year was out, Yenta gave birth to a baby girl and Lemel went to tell the Elder of Chelm the good tidings that a child had been born to them.

"Is the child a boy?" the Elder asked.

"No."

"Is it a girl?"

"How did you guess?" Lemel asked in amazement.

And the Elder of Chelm replied, "For the wise men of Chelm there are no secrets."

The First Shlemiel

THE FIRST SHLEMIEL

THERE ARE many shlemiels in the world, but the very first one came from the village of Chelm. He had a wife, Mrs. Shlemiel, and a child, Little Shlemiel, but he could not provide for them. His wife used to get up early in the morning to sell vegetables in the marketplace. Mr. Shlemiel stayed at home and rocked the baby to sleep. He also took care of the rooster which lived in the room with them, feeding it corn and water.

Mrs. Shlemiel knew that her husband was unhandy and lazy. He also loved to sleep and had a sweet tooth. It so happened that one night she prepared a potful of delicious jam. The next day she worried that while she was away at the market, her husband would eat it all up. So before she left, she said to him, "Shlemiel, I'm going to the market and I will be back in the evening. There are three things that I want to tell you. Each one is very important."

"What are they?" asked Shlemiel.

"First, make sure that the baby does not fall out of his cradle."

"Good. I will take care of the baby."

"Secondly, don't let the rooster get out of the house."

"Good. The rooster won't get out of the house."

"Thirdly, there is a potful of poison on the shelf. Be careful not to eat it, or you will die," said Mrs. Shlemiel, pointing to the pot of jam she had placed high up in the cupboard.

She had decided to fool him, because she knew that once he tasted the delicious jam, he would not stop eating until the pot was empty. It was just before Hanukkah, and she needed the jam to serve with the holiday pancakes.

As soon as his wife left, Shlemiel began to rock the baby and to sing him a lullaby:

> *I am a big Shlemiel.*
> *You are a little Shlemiel.*
> *When you grow up,*
> *You will be a big Shlemiel*
> *And I will be an old Shlemiel.*
> *When you have children,*
> *You will be a papa Shlemiel*
> *And I will be a grandpa Shlemiel.*

The baby soon fell asleep and Shlemiel dozed too, still rocking the cradle with his foot.

Shlemiel dreamed that he had become the richest man in Chelm. He was so rich that he could eat pancakes with jam not only on Hanukkah but every day of the year. He spent all day with the other wealthy men of Chelm playing games with a golden dreidel. Shlemiel knew a trick, and whenever it was his turn to spin the dreidel, it fell on the winning "G." He grew so famous that nobles from distant countries came to him and said, "Shlemiel, we want you to be our king."

Shlemiel told them he did not want to be a king. But the nobles fell on their knees before him and insisted until he had to agree. They placed a crown on his head and led him to a golden throne. Mrs. Shlemiel, now a queen, no longer needed to sell vegetables in the market. She sat next to him, and between them they shared a huge pancake spread with jam. He ate from one side and she from the other until their mouths met.

As Shlemiel sat and dreamed his sweet dream the rooster suddenly started crowing. It had a very strong voice. When it came out with a cock-a-doodle-doo, it rang like a bell. Now when a bell rang in Chelm, it usually meant there was a fire. Shlemiel awakened from his dream and jumped up in fright, overturning the cradle. The baby fell out and hurt his head. In his confusion Shlemiel ran to the window and opened it to see where the fire was. The moment he opened the window, the excited rooster flew out and hopped away.

Shlemiel called after it, "Rooster, you come back. If Mrs. Shlemiel finds you gone, she will rave and rant and I will never hear the end of it."

But the rooster paid no attention to Shlemiel. It didn't

even look back, and soon it had disappeared from sight.

When Shlemiel realized that there was no fire, he closed the window and went back to the crying baby, who by this time had a big bump on his forehead from the fall. With great effort Shlemiel comforted the baby, righted the cradle, and put him back into it.

Again he began to rock the cradle and sing a song:

In my dream I was a rich Shlemiel
But awake I am a poor Shlemiel.
In my dream I ate pancakes with jam;
Awake I chew bread and onion.
In my dream I was Shlemiel the King
But awake I'm just Shlemiel.

Having finally sung the baby to sleep, Shlemiel began to worry about his troubles. He knew that when his wife returned and found the rooster gone and the baby with a bump on his head, she would be beside herself with anger. Mrs. Shlemiel had a very loud voice, and when she scolded and screamed, poor Shlemiel trembled with fear. Shlemiel could foresee that tonight, when she got home, his wife would be angrier than ever before and would berate him and call him names.

Suddenly Shlemiel said to himself, "What is the sense of such a life? I'd rather be dead." And he decided to end his life. But how to do it? He then remembered what his wife had told him in the morning about the pot of poison that stood on the shelf. "That's what I will do. I will poison myself. When I'm dead she can revile me as much as she likes. A dead Shlemiel does not hear when he is screamed at."

Shlemiel was a short man and he could not reach the shelf. He got a stool, climbed up on it, took down the pot, and began to eat.

"Oh, the poison tastes sweet," he said to himself. He had heard that some poisons have a bitter taste and others are sweet. "But," he reasoned, "sweet poison is better than bitter," and proceeded to finish up the jam. It tasted so good, he licked the pot clean.

After Shlemiel had finished the pot of poison, he lay down on the bed. He was sure that the poison would soon begin to burn his insides and that he would die. But half an hour passed and then an hour, and Shlemiel lay without a single pain in his belly.

"This poison works very slowly," Shlemiel decided. He was thirsty and wanted a drink of water, but there was no water in the house. In Chelm water had to be fetched from an outside well, and Shlemiel was too lazy to go and get it.

Shlemiel remembered that his wife was saving a bottle of apple cider for the holidays. Apple cider was expensive, but when a man is about to die, what is the point of saving money? Shlemiel got out the bottle of cider and drank it down to the last drop.

Now Shlemiel began to have an ache in his stomach, and he was sure that the poison had begun to work. Convinced that he was about to die, he said to himself, "It's not really so bad to die. With such poison I wouldn't mind dying every day." And he dozed off.

He dreamed again that he was a king. He wore three crowns on his head, one on top of the other. Before him stood three golden pots: one filled with pancakes, one with jam, and one with apple cider. Whenever he soiled his beard with eating, a servant wiped it for him with a napkin.

Mrs. Shlemiel, the queen, sat next to him on her separate throne and said, "Of all the kings who ever ruled in Chelm, you are the greatest. The whole of Chelm pays homage to your wisdom. Fortunate is the queen of such a king. Happy is the prince who has you as a father."

Shlemiel was awakened by the sound of the door creaking open. The room was dark and he heard his wife's screechy voice. "Shlemiel, why didn't you light the lamp?"

"It sounds like my wife, Mrs. Shlemiel," Shlemiel said to himself. "But how is it possible that I hear her voice? I happen to be dead. Or can it be that the poison hasn't worked yet and I am still alive?" He got up, his legs shaking, and saw his wife lighting the lamp.

Suddenly she began to scream at the top of her lungs. "Just look at the baby! He has a bump on his head. Shlemiel, where is the rooster, and who drank the apple cider? Woe is me! He drank up the cider! He lost the rooster and let the baby get a bump on his head. Shlemiel, what have you done?"

"Don't scream, dear wife. I'm about to die. You will soon be a widow."

"Die? Widow? What are you talking about? You look healthy as a horse."

"I've poisoned myself," Shlemiel replied.

"Poisoned? What do you mean?" asked Mrs. Shlemiel.

"I've eaten your potful of poison."

And Shlemiel pointed to the empty pot of jam.

62

"Poison?" said Mrs. Shlemiel. "That's my pot of jam for Hanukkah."

"But you told me it was poison," Shlemiel insisted.

"You fool," she said. "I did that to keep you from eating it before the holiday. Now you've swallowed the whole potful." And Mrs. Shlemiel burst out crying.

Shlemiel too began to cry, but not from sorrow. He wept tears of joy that he would remain alive. The wailing of the parents woke the baby and he too began to yowl. When the neighbors heard all the crying, they came running and soon all of Chelm knew the story. The good neighbors took pity on the Shlemiels and brought them a fresh pot of jam and another bottle of apple cider. The rooster, which had gotten cold and hungry from wandering around outside, returned by itself and the Shlemiels had a happy holiday after all.

As always in Chelm when an unusual event occurred, the Elders came together to ponder over what had happened. For seven days and seven nights they sat wrinkling their foreheads and tugging at their beards, searching for the true meaning of the incident. At the end the sages all came to the same conclusion: A wife who has a child in the cradle and a rooster to take care of should never lie to her husband and tell him that a pot of jam is a pot of poison, or that a pot of poison is a pot of jam, even if he is lazy, has a sweet tooth, and is a shlemiel besides.

The Devil's Trick

THE DEVIL'S TRICK

THE SNOW had been falling for three days and three nights. Houses were snowed in and windowpanes covered with frost flowers. The wind whistled in the chimneys. Gusts of snow somersaulted in the cold air.

The devil's wife rode on her hoop, with a broom in one hand and a rope in the other. Before her ran a white goat with a black beard and twisted horns. Behind her strode the devil with his cobweb face, holes instead of eyes, hair to his shoulders, and legs as long as stilts.

In a one-room hut, with a low ceiling and soot-covered walls, sat David, a poor boy with a pale face and black eyes. He was alone with his baby brother on the first night of Hanukkah. His father had gone to the village to buy corn, but three days had passed and he had not returned home. David's mother had gone to look for her husband, and she too had not come back.

The baby slept in his cradle. In the Hanukkah lamp flickered the first candle, which David himself had lit.

David was so worried he could not stay home any longer. He put on his padded coat and his cap with earlaps, made sure that the baby was covered, and went out to look for his parents.

That was what the devil had been waiting for. He immediately whipped up the storm. Black clouds covered the sky. David could hardly see in the thick darkness. The frost burned his face. The snow fell dry and heavy as salt. The wind caught David by his coattails and tried to lift him up off the ground. He was surrounded by laughter, as if from a thousand imps.

David realized the goblins were after him. He tried to turn back and go home, but he could not find his way. The snow and darkness swallowed *everything*. It became clear to him that the devils must have caught his parents. Would they get him also? But heaven and earth have vowed that the devil may never succeed completely in his tricks. No matter how shrewd the devil is, he will always make a mistake, especially on Hanukkah.

The powers of evil had managed to hide the stars, but they could not extinguish the single Hanukkah candle. David saw its light and ran toward it. The devil ran after him. The devil's wife followed on her hoop, yelling and waving her broom, trying to lasso him with her rope. David ran even more quickly than they, and reached the hut just ahead of the devil. As David opened the door the devil tried to get in with him. David managed to slam the door behind him. In the rush and struggle the devil's tail got stuck in the door.

"Give me back my tail," the devil screamed.

And David replied, "Give me back my father and mother."

The devil swore that he knew nothing about them, but David did not let himself be fooled.

"You kidnapped them, cursed Devil," David said. He picked up a sharp ax and told the devil that he would cut off his tail.

"Have pity on me. I have only one tail," the devil cried. And to his wife he said, "Go quickly to the cave behind the black mountains and bring back the man and woman we led astray."

His wife sped away on her hoop and soon brought the couple back. David's father sat on the hoop holding on to the witch by her hair; his mother came riding on the white goat, its black beard clasped tightly in her hands.

"Your mother and father are here. Give me my tail," said the devil.

David looked through the keyhole and saw his parents were really there. He wanted to open the door at once and let them in, but he was not yet ready to free the devil.

He rushed over to the window, took the Hanukkah candle, and singed the devil's tail. "Now, Devil, you will always remember," he cried, "Hanukkah is no time for making trouble."

Then at last he opened the door. The devil licked his singed tail and ran off with his wife to the land where no people walk, no cattle tread, where the sky is copper and the earth is iron.

73

Zlateh The Goat

ZLATEH THE GOAT

AT HANUKKAH time the road from the village to the town is usually covered with snow, but this year the winter had been a mild one. Hanukkah had almost come, yet little snow had fallen. The sun shone most of the time. The peasants complained that because of the dry weather there would be a poor harvest of winter grain. New grass sprouted, and the peasants sent their cattle out to pasture.

For Reuven the furrier it was a bad year, and after long hesitation he decided to sell Zlateh the goat. She was old and gave little milk. Feyvel the town butcher had offered eight gulden for her. Such a sum would buy Hanukkah candles, potatoes and oil for pancakes, gifts for the children, and other holiday necessaries for the house. Reuven told his oldest boy Aaron to take the goat to town.

Aaron understood what taking the goat to Feyvel meant, but he had to obey his father. Leah, his mother, wiped the tears from her eyes when she heard the news. Aaron's younger sisters, Anna and Miriam, cried loudly. Aaron put on his quilted jacket and a cap with earmuffs, bound a rope around Zlateh's neck, and took along two slices of bread with cheese to eat on the road. Aaron was supposed to deliver the goat by evening, spend the night at the butcher's, and return the next day with the money.

While the family said good-bye to the goat, and Aaron placed the rope around her neck, Zlateh stood as patiently and good-naturedly as ever. She licked Reuven's hand. She shook her small white beard. Zlateh trusted human beings. She knew that they always fed her and never did her any harm.

When Aaron brought her out on the road to town, she seemed somewhat astonished. She'd never been led in that direction before. She looked back at him questioningly, as if to say, "Where are you taking me?" But after a while she seemed to come to the conclusion that a goat shouldn't ask questions. Still, the road was different. They passed new fields, pastures, and huts with thatched roofs. Here and there a dog barked and came running after them, but Aaron chased it away with his stick.

The sun was shining when Aaron left the village. Suddenly the weather changed. A large black cloud with a bluish center appeared in the east and spread itself rapidly over the sky. A cold wind blew in with it. The crows flew low, croaking. At first it looked as if it would rain, but

80

instead it began to hail as in summer. It was early in the day, but it became dark as dusk. After a while the hail turned to snow.

In his twelve years Aaron had seen all kinds of weather, but he had never experienced a snow like this one. It was so dense it shut out the light of the day. In a short time their path was completely covered. The wind became as cold as ice. The road to town was narrow and winding. Aaron no longer knew where he was. He could not see through the snow. The cold soon penetrated his quilted jacket.

At first Zlateh didn't seem to mind the change in weather. She too was twelve years old and knew what winter meant. But when her legs sank deeper and deeper into the snow, she began to turn her head and look at Aaron in wonderment. Her mild eyes seemed to ask, "Why are we out in such a storm?" Aaron hoped that a peasant would come along with his cart, but no one passed by.

The snow grew thicker, falling to the ground in large, whirling flakes. Beneath it Aaron's boots touched the softness of a plowed field. He realized that he was no longer on the road. He had gone astray. He could no longer figure out which was east or west, which way was the village, the town. The wind whistled, howled, whirled the snow about in eddies. It looked as if white imps were playing tag on the fields. A white dust rose above the ground. Zlateh stopped. She could walk no longer. Stubbornly she anchored her cleft hooves in the earth and bleated as if pleading to be taken home. Icicles hung from her white beard, and her horns were glazed with frost.

Aaron did not want to admit the danger, but he knew

just the same that if they did not find shelter they would freeze to death. This was no ordinary storm. It was a mighty blizzard. The snowfall had reached his knees. His hands were numb, and he could no longer feel his toes. He choked when he breathed. His nose felt like wood, and he rubbed it with snow. Zlateh's bleating began to sound like crying. Those humans in whom she had so much confidence had dragged her into a trap. Aaron began to pray to God for himself and for the innocent animal.

Suddenly he made out the shape of a hill. He wondered what it could be. Who had piled snow into such a huge heap? He moved toward it, dragging Zlateh after him. When he came near it, he realized that it was a large hay-stack which the snow had blanketed.

Aaron realized immediately that they were saved. With great effort he dug his way through the snow. He was a village boy and knew what to do. When he reached the hay, he hollowed out a nest for himself and the goat. No matter how cold it may be outside, in the hay it is always warm. And hay was food for Zlateh. The moment she smelled it she became contented and began to eat. Outside the snow continued to fall. It quickly covered the passage-way Aaron had dug. But a boy and an animal need to breathe, and there was hardly any air in their hideout. Aaron bored a kind of a window through the hay and snow and carefully kept the passage clear.

Zlateh, having eaten her fill, sat down on her hind legs and seemed to have regained her confidence in man. Aaron ate his two slices of bread and cheese, but after the difficult journey he was still hungry. He looked at Zlateh and

noticed her udders were full. He lay down next to her, placing himself so that when he milked her he could squirt the milk into his mouth. It was rich and sweet. Zlateh was not accustomed to being milked that way, but she did not resist. On the contrary, she seemed eager to reward Aaron for bringing her to a shelter whose very walls, floor, and ceiling were made of food.

Through the window Aaron could catch a glimpse of the chaos outside. The wind carried before it whole drifts of snow. It was completely dark, and he did not know whether night had already come or whether it was the darkness of the storm. Thank God that in the hay it was not cold. The dried hay, grass, and field flowers exuded the warmth of the summer sun. Zlateh ate frequently; she nibbled from above, below, from the left and right. Her body gave forth an animal warmth, and Aaron cuddled up to her. He had always loved Zlateh, but now she was like a sister. He was alone, cut off from his family, and wanted to talk. He began to talk to Zlateh. "Zlateh, what do you think about what has happened to us?" he asked.

"Maaaa," Zlateh answered.

"If we hadn't found this stack of hay, we would both be frozen stiff by now," Aaron said.

"Maaaa," was the goat's reply.

"If the snow keeps on falling like this, we may have to stay here for days," Aaron explained.

"Maaaa," Zlateh bleated.

"What does 'Maaaa' mean?" Aaron asked. "You'd better speak up clearly."

"Maaaa. Maaaa," Zlateh tried.

85

"Well, let it be 'Maaaa' then," Aaron said patiently. "You can't speak, but I know you understand. I need you and you need me. Isn't that right?"

"Maaaa."

Aaron became sleepy. He made a pillow out of some hay, leaned his head on it, and dozed off. Zlateh too fell asleep.

When Aaron opened his eyes, he didn't know whether it was morning or night. The snow had blocked up his window. He tried to clear it, but when he had bored through to the length of his arm, he still hadn't reached the outside. Luckily he had his stick with him and was able to break through to the open air. It was still dark outside. The snow continued to fall and the wind wailed, first with one voice and then with many. Sometimes it had the sound of devilish laughter. Zlateh too awoke, and when Aaron greeted her, she answered, "Maaaa." Yes, Zlateh's language consisted of only one word, but it meant many things. Now she was saying, "We must accept all that God gives us—heat, cold, hunger, satisfaction, light, and darkness."

Aaron had awakened hungry. He had eaten up his food, but Zlateh had plenty of milk.

For three days Aaron and Zlateh stayed in the haystack. Aaron had always loved Zlateh, but in these three days he loved her more and more. She fed him with her milk and helped him keep warm. She comforted him with her patience. He told her many stories, and she always cocked her ears and listened. When he patted her, she licked his hand and his face. Then she said, "Maaaa," and he knew it meant, I love you too.

86

The snow fell for three days, though after the first day it was not as thick and the wind quieted down. Sometimes Aaron felt that there could never have been a summer, that the snow had always fallen, ever since he could remember. He, Aaron, never had a father or mother or sisters. He was a snow child, born of the snow, and so was Zlateh. It was so quiet in the hay that his ears rang in the stillness. Aaron and Zlateh slept all night and a good part of the day. As for Aaron's dreams, they were all about warm weather. He dreamed of green fields, trees covered with blossoms, clear brooks, and singing birds. By the third night the snow had stopped, but Aaron did not dare to find his way home in the darkness. The sky became clear and the moon shone, casting silvery nets on the snow. Aaron dug his way out and looked at the world. It was all white, quiet, dreaming dreams of heavenly splendor. The stars were large and close. The moon swam in the sky as in a sea.

On the morning of the fourth day Aaron heard the ringing of sleigh bells. The haystack was not far from the road. The peasant who drove the sleigh pointed out the way to him—not to the town and Feyvel the butcher, but home to the village. Aaron had decided in the haystack that he would never part with Zlateh.

Aaron's family and their neighbors had searched for the boy and the goat but had found no trace of them during the storm. They feared they were lost. Aaron's mother and sisters cried for him; his father remained silent and gloomy. Suddenly one of the neighbors came running to their house with the news that Aaron and Zlateh were coming up the road.

89

There was great joy in the family. Aaron told them how he had found the stack of hay and how Zlateh had fed him with her milk. Aaron's sisters kissed and hugged Zlateh and gave her a special treat of chopped carrots and potato peels, which Zlateh gobbled up hungrily.

Nobody ever again thought of selling Zlateh, and now that the cold weather had finally set in, the villagers needed the services of Reuven the furrier once more. When Hanukkah came, Aaron's mother was able to fry pancakes every evening, and Zlateh got her portion too. Even though Zlateh had her own pen, she often came to the kitchen, knocking on the door with her horns to indicate that she was ready to visit, and she was always admitted. In the evening Aaron, Miriam, and Anna played dreidel. Zlateh sat near the stove watching the children and the flickering of the Hanukkah candles.

Once in a while Aaron would ask her, "Zlateh, do you remember the three days we spent together?"

And Zlateh would scratch her neck with a horn, shake her white bearded head and come out with the single sound which expressed all her thoughts, and all her love.